KS3

Return Descender

Robin and Chris Lawrie

Illustrated by
Robin Lawrie

Acknowledgements

The authors and publishers would like to thank
Julia Francis, Hereford Diocesan Deaf Church
lay co-chaplain, for her help with the sign language
in the *Chain Gang* books.

Return Descender **is based on a idea by Kate Lawrie.**

Published by Evans Brothers Limited
2A Portman Mansions
Chiltern Street
London W1U 6NR

© Robin and Christine Lawrie

First published 2001

The authors assert their moral right to be identified as the
authors of this work in accordance with the Copyright, Designs
and Patents Act, 1988.

Printed in Hong Kong

British Library Cataloguing in Publication data.
Lawrie, Robin
  Return Descender. – (The Chain Gang)
  1. Slam Duncan (Fictitious character) – Juvenile fiction
  2. All terrain cycling – Juvenile fiction 3. Adventure stories
  4. Children's stories
  I. Title II. Lawrie, Chris
  823.9'14[J]

ISBN 0 237 52262 4

Hi! My name is "Slam" Duncan. I ride and race downhill mountain bikes with a group of kids called "The Chain Gang".

I'm Aziz, but people call me "Dozy."

I'm Fionn.

I'm Larry.

We are in training for the "Sword in the Stump" series of mountain bike races. The race organisers are trying to promote good sportsmanship and fair play between young off-road riders. The next two races are duel descenders where two people race down a tough, off-road course together. It's hairy, but fun.

* I'm Andy. (Andy is deaf and uses sign language.)

5

Duel descender bikes need a super-strong,
rigid frame, a small, single-ring
chain wheel for fast sprints and
heavy-duty shock absorbers
to soak up high-speed
bumps. They are
very pricey.

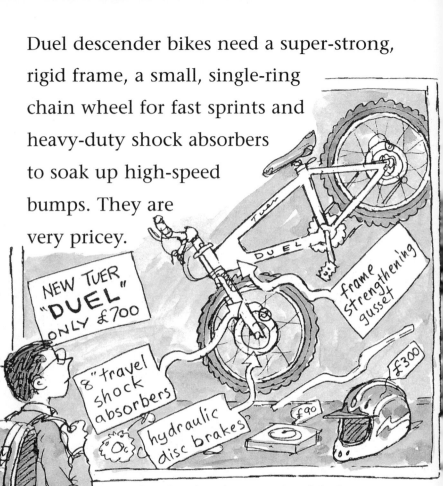

NEW TUER
"DUEL"
ONLY £700

frame
strengthening
gusset

8" travel
shock
absorbers

hydraulic
disc brakes

£300

£90

I had a look at a duel bike
in Tuer Cycles shop window.

Hopeless! I earn
racing money by
working in my
dad's garage . . .

6

. . . but he doesn't pay much. Sometimes, though, he's a pal. After I had explained my problem, he said:

OK. You've already got an old, cross-country rigid frame and a downhill bike with big shock absorbers. Let's just stick the two together.

No good. The heavy downhill shocks will break the old frame.

Leave it to me!

Dad got out the welding torch and in minutes had welded

BZZTT! SSSPFF!

massive frame strengtheners on to my rigid cross-country frame. I bolted on the downhill shocks. Result: ugly but fast.

The Sword in the Stump race series
is supposed to encourage good
sportsmanship in juvenile
riders. But I had done
badly in the first
cross-country race
and had kind of
forgotten
that.

As a gang,
we always
practise together so nobody gets
an unfair advantage, but I was desperate.
I had never done a duel descender,
so I decided to do some
solo practice.

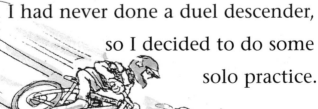

My new hybrid was really flying.

Suddenly, I heard someone behind me.
It was Andy. He, too, was
getting in some
quiet practice.

We both
stopped at the
same time.

It was daft practising alone for a
two-person event anyway, so we decided
to join forces. Andy explained the rules:

1. Nudging 2. OK 3 with knees 4. and
elbows 5. but keep hands on handlebars.

*What are you doing here? ** And you?

We spent the morning practising overtaking . . .

. . . nudging . . .

. . . dogging it . . .

. . . and CRASHING!

Unlike me,
Andy had done duel descenders before.
He was a great teacher, and carefully
explained about getting away fast,
braking late, and getting to the
first corner in front.

I was ready to rock!

After our practice, my new bike
needed a clean up.
I found what I
thought was an
old rag by the
laundry
basket.

I gave the bike a good wash and polish.

Then I went round to see Dozy.

He told me that he, Larry and

Fionn were not going to do
the duel descender races because they
did not have the right bikes.
Bad news.
But when I got home,
Sis gave me some
REALLY bad news.

13

I was GUTTED!

The race was the next day.

Too late to do anything.

Somehow, Andy got to know about it.
He came round
with some rigid forks
and old wheels.
He helped me bolt them on to my
downhill frame.
It was ugly and slow, but
I would be racing tomorrow!

● ● ●

A duel descender course is like
a downhill course
with rocks, roots
and jumps, but
not as long.
You're not racing against
the clock, either.
You're racing
against another
person.

START

Flyover

1st jump

Black Hole

FINISH

16

Race day. 10 a.m. There I was, up against
my arch rival, "Punk" Tuer,
and I was on the wrong
bike for the job. I tried to
remember everything
that Andy had told me.
Then the starting gate
crashed to the ground.

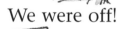

We were off!

At the flyover,
we were neck
and neck.

At the first jump,
we were
side by side.

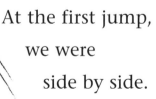

But we were
almost at . . .

17

. . . THE BLACK HOLE!

This is a nasty, high-speed
spiral, wide enough
for two at the top,
but with room
for only one
at the
bottom.

Somehow,
I forced
my way
ahead of Punk.
But not far enough.

18

I felt a hand shove
me in the back.
Andy had told me
it was illegal to do that
and your hands must stay on the bars!

Luckily for Punk, none of the marshalls saw it. Unluckily for me . . .

. . . I went butt over biscuit, straight over the edge.

Somehow, I walked away from it.
Straight home.
I couldn't bear to stay
and watch Punk's next ride.

creak
creak

So unfair! If I'd had my duel bike, he wouldn't have got near me.

• • •

I knew I would have to get my proper
bike back from Steady Eddy, or my
Sword in the Stump challenge was over.
I asked Sis for his 'phone number.

Please.

GET LOST!

GIRLY

Once more, it was Andy to the rescue.
For some reason, he had Eddy's mobile
number. I didn't ask why.
He sent Eddy
a text message.

can u meet Slam 2 day

A reply
came back.

Smith St. market B43

I got there just before 3 o'clock.

Eddy was selling "secondhand" bikes off the back of his pickup.

OK, Eddy, where's my duel bike?

It's not your bike any more, kid. I sold it. Now, GO AWAY!

Eddy's mates looked a bit like gorillas, so I did just that.

I took the long way home through Shredbury Park, when suddenly:

Hey, Slam, you should have stuck around to see me win yesterday.

It was Pete Plank and he was riding. . .

MY DUEL BIKE!

He had resprayed it but I would know Dad's welding anywhere.

That's my bike!

No, it's not. My dad bought it for me.

GIVE IT BACK!

IF YOU WANT IT COME AND GET IT!

So the chase was on, out of the park and . . .

23

I never did catch him.

Next Saturday; second round of the duels; first heat 10 a.m. Once more I was drawn against Punk. 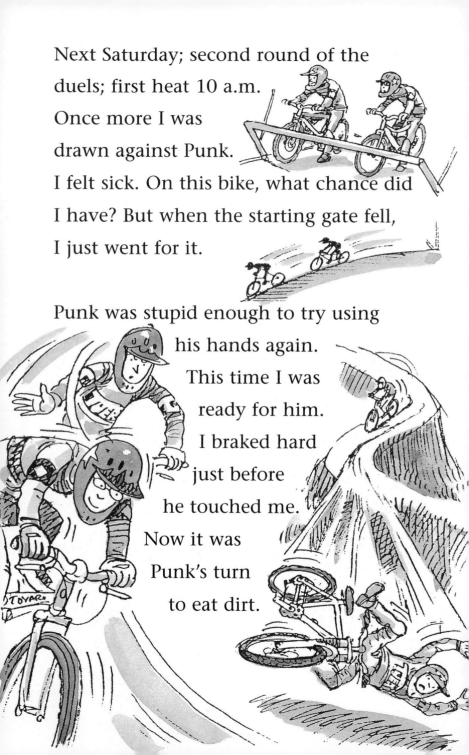 I felt sick. On this bike, what chance did I have? But when the starting gate fell, I just went for it.

Punk was stupid enough to try using his hands again. This time I was ready for him. I braked hard just before he touched me. Now it was Punk's turn to eat dirt.

In my next heat I was
up against Punk's mate,
"Dyno" Sawyer.
He messed up
a jump.

AAARGHH!

My next opponent was Andy. He would
be hard to beat. But he had been looking
green all morning.

Harry's Burgers

He'd had one of
Harry's famous greaseburgers for breakfast.
We were only
halfway down
when Andy
lost his breakfast,
and the race.

* Problems? ** I'll say!

27

The next race would be the final. And I would be racing Pete Plank. I felt like finding him and telling him to hand over my bike. Then I thought of the Sword in the Stump and what it meant. Pete's dad had bought my bike fair and square. I decided to keep my mouth shut.

• • •

Then I started to think about how much Andy had helped me get ready for the race. And then I had gone and beaten him. I went to look for him instead.

I found him and signed:

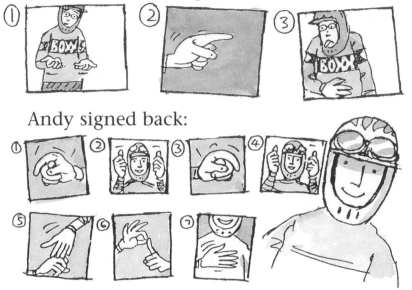

Andy signed back:

So I decided to do just that.

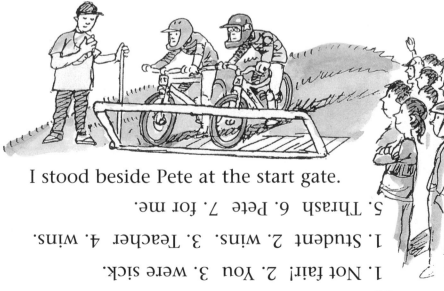

I stood beside Pete at the start gate.

5. Thrash 6. Pete 7. for me.

1. Student 2. wins. 3. Teacher 4. wins.

1. Not fair! 2. You 3. were sick.

But it was jammed. I looked around and saw Andy in the crowd. He was signing something else.

COME ON! HURRY UP!

"Pete injured. Left arm. Won't nudge that side. Overtake on lefthand bend."

A second later we were off. Pete was way out in front through the flyover.

At the first set of double jumps he could not resist showing off. A bad landing slowed him down long enough for me to get past.

But I couldn't make it stick.

The next bend was a left-hander. It was so-o-o easy. I just took him on the inside. I won the race . . .

. . . and had a lovely wodge of prize money to prove it.

Got to find Pete and buy my bike back. I'll need its frame and forks for the next three races!

He was happy to take my money.

That's the last duel race in the stump series anyway. Here, you're welcome to it.

Just then, I saw Andy.

I signed:

He signed back:

Then I signed:

7. No way! 8. Greaseburgers! 9. Yuk!

4. You'd do 5 the same 6. for me.

1. Cheers, mate. 2. You've been 3. a pal.